WE BOTH READ®

Parent's Introduction

We Both Read is the first series of books designed to invite parents and children to share the reading of a story by taking turns reading aloud. This "shared reading" innovation, which was developed with reading education specialists, invites parents to read the more complex text and storyline on the left-hand pages. Then, children can be encouraged to read the right-hand pages, which feature less complex text and storyline, specifically written for the beginning reader.

Reading aloud is one of the most important activities parents can share with their child to assist them in their reading development. However, *We Both Read* goes beyond reading *to* a child and allows parents to share the reading *with* a child. *We Both Read* is so powerful and effective because it combines two key elements in learning: "modeling" (the parent reads) and "doing" (the child reads). The result is not only faster reading development for the child, but a much more enjoyable and enriching experience for both!

You may find it helpful to read the entire book aloud yourself the first time, then invite your child to participate in the second reading. In some books, a few more difficult words will first be introduced in the parent's text, distinguished with **bold lettering**. Pointing out, and even discussing, these words will help familiarize your child with them and help to build your child's vocabulary. Also, note that a "talking parent" icon ☺ precedes the parent's text and a "talking child" icon ☺ precedes the child's text.

We encourage you to share and interact with your child as you read the book together. If your child is having difficulty, you might want to mention a few things to help them. "Sounding out" is good, but it will not work with all words. Children can pick up clues about the words they are reading from the story, the context of the sentence, or even the pictures. Some stories have rhyming patterns that might help. It might also help them to touch the words with their finger as they read, to better connect the voice sound and the printed word.

Sharing the *We Both Read* books together will engage you and your child in an interactive adventure in reading! It is a fun and easy way to encourage and help your child to read—and a wonderful way to start them off on a lifetime of reading enjoyment!

We Both Read: Frank and the Balloon

Text Copyright ©2007 by Dev Ross
Illustrations Copyright ©2007 Larry Reinhart
All rights reserved

We Both Read® is a trademark of Treasure Bay, Inc.

Published by Treasure Bay, Inc.
40 Sir Francis Drake Boulevard
San Anselmo, CA 94960 USA

PRINTED IN SINGAPORE

Library of Congress Catalog Card Number: 2007920850

Hardcover ISBN-10: 1-60115-011-3
Hardcover ISBN-13: 978-1-60115-011-0
Paperback ISBN-10: 1-60115-012-1
Paperback ISBN-13: 978-1-60115-012-7

We Both Read® Books
Patent No. 5,957,693

Visit us online at:
www.webothread.com

Frank
and the Balloon

By Dev Ross

Illustrated by Larry Reinhart

TREASURE BAY

Frank the frog likes to play. He likes to play with his best friend, Mikey the mouse. One day, he and Mikey were playing on . . .

. . . the swing.

 Mikey didn't want to swing too high.
Swinging too high made him feel afraid,
but not Frank. Frank wanted to swing up
as high as he could. He wanted to swing
up as high as . . .

. . . an airplane.

Frank was just thinking how fun it would be to fly in an airplane when something red whooshed past them. The red thing twirled in the air on a gust of wind, then dove out of the sky and disappeared behind some very . . .

. . . tall grass.

Frank and Mikey hurried to the grass to find the red thing. Mikey was afraid it might be something scary, but not Frank. Since it seemed to come from up in **space,** Frank was hoping the red thing was a . . .

. . . **space** man.

Frank parted the grass and saw two square
eyes, a rectangular nose, and a smiling mouth,
but they did not belong to a space man. The
two square eyes, the rectangular nose, and
the smiling mouth were painted on . . .

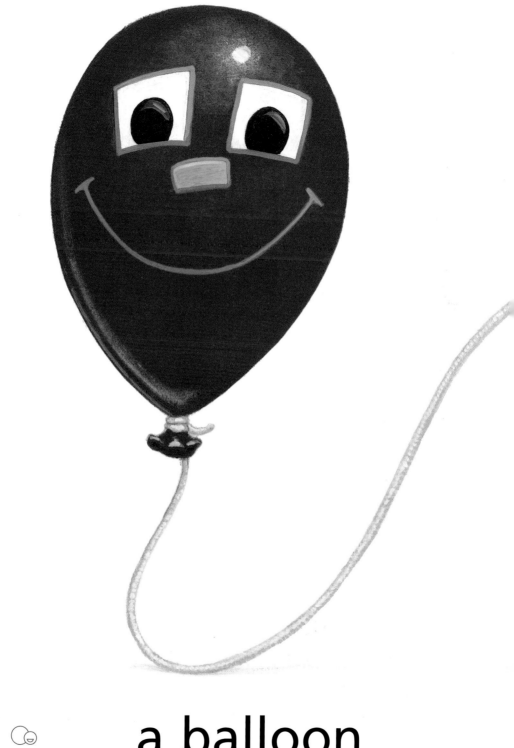

. . . a balloon.

The balloon had a long string tied to it. The string was tangled around a yellow dandelion. The tangled string was holding the balloon down. Frank untangled the string and the balloon floated . . .

. . . up!

Frank was so busy watching the balloon float up that he forgot he was holding its string. Now he was floating up too!

"Let go!" cried Mikey. He was feeling very worried for Frank. He wanted Frank to let go of the balloon's long, dangling . . .

 . . . string.

☺ Frank wanted to let go, but when he looked
down he could see the ground getting further
and further away. So, Frank politely asked the
balloon to go down. It did not go down.
Instead, it floated even higher into . . .

 . . . the sky.

From high in the sky, Frank could see wonderful things below him. He could see the pond where he lived. He could see the tops of trees. He could even see Mikey, who was his very best . . .

. . . friend.

👓 "Come back, Frank!" shouted Mikey.

Frank, however, did not want to go back. He wanted to be the first frog to travel around the whole wide world. He wanted to be the first frog . . .

... to fly.

Mikey didn't want his best friend to fly. In fact, he didn't want him to stay up in the sky a single minute longer.

"Frogs should not be so high up!" Mikey scolded. "Frogs should be down here. You should . . .

. . . come down!"

 "Don't worry, Mikey! I like being up here!" said Frank.

Then all of a sudden . . . WHOOSH! The balloon and Frank were carried up even higher by a blustery gust . . .

. . . of wind.

"Whee!" cried Frank.

"Oh, no!" wailed Mikey.

"Moo!" called out another voice from below.

Frank looked down and saw that he was
floating right over Betty, . . .

... the cow.

Betty, the cow, was very surprised when Mikey jumped on her back.

"Follow that balloon!" roared Mikey.

Betty the cow **ran** after the balloon. **She** did not run slowly.

She ran fast!

Meanwhile, Frank said hello to a passing bird. He winked at a buzzing bumble bee. He waved at a beautiful . . .

. . . butterfly.